This book belongs to:

_____

Lucy and Lilo
Help the Honu

story and illustrations by
Mary Kate Wright

Mutual Publishing

For my Mom,
with love.

ISBN-10: 1-56647-926-6
ISBN-13: 978-1-56647-926-4
Library of Congress Cataloging
information available upon request

Design by Jane Gillespie
First Printing, September 2010

Mutual Publishing, LLC
1215 Center Street, Suite 210
Honolulu, Hawaii 96816
Ph: (808) 732-1709
Fax: (808) 734-4094
e-mail: info@mutualpublishing.com
www.mutualpublishing.com

Printed in China

Today begins like any other day. It's a typical Hawaiian morning with the sun shining, the trade winds blowing, and the sweet scent of plumeria in the air.

But for Lucy and Lilo, the day will be far from ordinary....

Time to go to the beach! Lucy and Lilo hear the jingle of their leashes. They race each other to the door. Their short walk to the beach takes twice as long because Lilo stops to scratch her back on the long grass. Lucy stops to inspect every bug they pass. As they near the beach, they tug on their leashes, anxious to get there.

Unleashed, they run for the water. Lucy leaps gracefully over the waves. Lilo follows but runs straight into a wave and swallows a mouthful of water. She jumps back up, shakes, and swims after Lucy.

After a quick swim, Lilo puts her nose close to the sand. She sniffs and explores all the shells, coconuts, and driftwood along the shore. Lucy snatches up a tennis ball, ready to play fetch.

Both Lucy and Lilo chase the ball to a deserted area down the beach. As they look for the ball, they discover a round patch of sand. Forgetting about the tennis ball, they circle the mysterious spot and sniff eagerly. It smells musty. Lucy starts to dig and dig. Sand flies everywhere!

They soon uncover a pile of small eggs that look like ping-pong balls. Lucy gently paws at one of the eggs while Lilo smells them excitedly. One of the eggs begins to wiggle and move. Lucy and Lilo jump back, startled. As the egg cracks open, a tiny honu pushes its way out into the light just as the other eggs begin to shift and crack. Before they know it, all of the eggs have cracked open and there's a pile of baby honu climbing over each other in the sand pit.

The honu scramble out of the hole and start to slip, slide, and wiggle their way toward the ocean. Lucy and Lilo are thrilled with their tiny, wiggly new friends. They run up and down the beach beside the turtle parade, careful not to step on any of the babies. They bark and chase away curious seabirds.

Soon the honu reach the water's edge. One by one, the hatchlings enter the ocean as Lucy and Lilo stand on the shore to watch their new friends swim away.

After they see all the honu bobbing up and down in the waves, Lucy and Lilo turn from the water and see something moving by the empty eggshells. They run over and find one last baby honu still struggling in the sand. The little turtle looks up at Lucy and Lilo, her small mouth opening and closing. All of her siblings are gone and she seems scared of being left behind.

Lilo bows her head and nudges the tiny honu with her nose. Lucy moves around to help. Together, they scoot the baby honu closer to the ocean with their noses while she paddles her flippers furiously in the sand. In no time at all, the last baby honu reaches the water's edge and slips in with a receding wave.

Lucy and Lilo watch her swim away. The journey from the nest to the ocean is the first of many challenges the honu will face in their lifetimes. Lucy and Lilo have helped at least one begin her journey. As they turn away from the water, Lucy remembers the tennis ball and they take off, running down the beach.

Later, Lucy and Lilo walk home, worn out, tired, and happy after an adventurous day at the beach.

The end.

The turtles that Lucy and Lilo helped are Hawaiian Green Sea Turtles. Honu (pronounced hoe-new) is the name for these turtles in the Hawaiian language. They are endangered species and are protected by the federal and state governments.

The nest of eggs Lucy and Lilo found is called a clutch. Each clutch usually contains about one hundred eggs buried in the sand. The hatchlings in a clutch are either all male or all female. Imagine having that many brothers or sisters!

Baby honu usually weigh one ounce—about the same weight as a slice of bread. When they hatch, their shells are dark green or black and about two inches long.

After digging out of their nest, the honu hatchlings must reach the water before being eaten by birds or hungry crabs, or overheating from the sun. Once in the ocean, they are hunted by sharks and other predatory fish. Only a small number of honu from each clutch reaches maturity.

The surviving baby honu are carried into the open ocean by the currents. Here they grow for several years, feeding on jellyfish and small invertebrates (animals with no backbone), before returning to coastal areas.

As adults, honu can weigh up to five hundred pounds and can grow up to forty-five inches long! The adult's shell is usually grayish-brown with gold, yellow, and green swirls on it. Green sea turtles are named for the color of their bodies not the color of their shells.

Adult honu live in shallow coastal waters, eating algae and limu (Hawaiian seaweed). The honu will come up on beaches to bask in the sun and perhaps to get away from their one predator, the shark. If you ever see these turtles on the beach or in the water, it is important to remember not to approach them and never to touch them.

When it's time to lay her eggs, the female honu comes ashore at night on the same beach where she was born. She uses her flippers to dig a pit, lays her eggs, and then covers the nest back up with sand before returning to the ocean. The eggs sit for about forty-five days before the baby honu hatch, and the cycle begins all over again!

About the Author

Mary Kate Wright is a certified medical illustrator currently living in 'Ewa Beach, Hawai'i. She holds a Bachelor of Arts from Tulane University and a Masters of Science in Medical Illustration from the Medical College of Georgia. She received her certification in medical illustration in 2005 from the Association of Medical Illustrators.

In 2005 her husband, who is an officer in the United States Army, received new orders and they moved halfway across the globe to Hawai'i. After the move, Mary Kate began her own medical illustration business. Currently she is sole proprietor of MKIllustrations and has clients from all aspects of the medical and scientific community.

Mary Kate has just begun to delve into the world of children's books. She has recently illustrated a story for children dealing with leukemia titled, *"My Blood Brother, A Story About Childhood Leukemia."*

When not drawing, Mary Kate likes to go to the beach and go hiking with her husband and two dogs.